W9-ARA-423

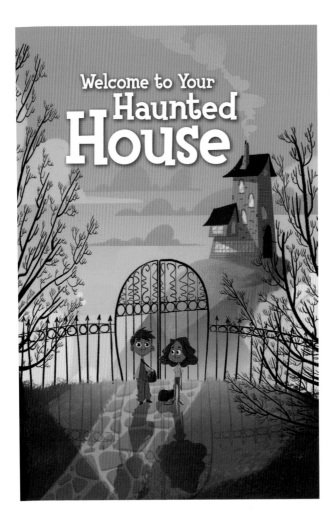

# Welcome to Your Haunted House

## By Gabrielle Snyder
## Illustrated by James Rey Sanchez

**Publishing Credits**

Rachelle Cracchiolo, M.S.Ed., *Publisher*
Conni Medina, M.A.Ed., *Editor in Chief*
Nika Fabienke, Ed.D., *Content Director*
Véronique Bos, *Creative Director*
Shaun N. Bernadou, *Art Director*
Carol Huey-Gatewood, M.A.Ed., *Editor*
Valerie Morales, *Associate Editor*
Kevin Pham, *Graphic Designer*

**Image Credits**

Illustrated by James Rey Sanchez

5301 Oceanus Drive
Huntington Beach, CA  92649-1030
www.tcmpub.com

**ISBN 978-1-6449-1325-3**
© 2020 Teacher Created Materials, Inc.

# Table of Contents

CHAPTER ONE

# Moving

Jason and I were at home playing our new favorite game called *try not to laugh*. I had him hiccup-laughing when Mom and Dad strolled into the family room. It's time for a family meeting," announced Mom.

"Uh-oh! What did you do this time, Jason?" I asked.

"No one is in trouble, Anna," said Mom, pushing her glasses to the top of her forehead. "We have some great news! We've bought a new house that's much closer to your school and our work, and we'll be moving as soon as we get everything packed up."

"It'll be an epic adventure for the whole family!" said Dad. "And you'll actually be able to walk to school every day."

"You're going to adore the new house," said Mom. "It's full of charm and, dare I say, mystery."

"There might even be some secret passageways for you to discover," said Dad.

I sighed and glanced at my big brother. He rolled his eyes. I could tell that he wasn't excited about the move either.

Later, while we were packing, I asked Jason, "Do you think there'll be anything fun to do at the new house?"

"I sincerely doubt it," he said. "I bet

there's no tree house or tire swing like we have here."

The day of the move, a gigantic moving truck pulled up in front of our house. While the movers loaded up, Jason and I wandered from room to room and then meandered out the back door into our yard.

"Goodbye, tire swing," said Jason, "I'm gonna miss you!"

We climbed the ladder up to our treehouse and surveyed our soon-to-be old domain.

We sat in silence, just listening to the crows cawing on the telephone wires, until Mom called us to leave. "Farewell, tree house," I whispered, climbing down the ladder for the last time.

As we pulled away from our old house, the sun sparkled at full wattage. But as we drove across town to the new house, dark clouds drifted across the sky, obstructing the sun.

We drove up a long, winding

hillside road.

"Spooky," said Jason.

I laughed nervously.

Finally, we pulled up to the new house—an ancient Victorian. It was a dingy gray with trim that might've been white a century or so ago.

Dad said, "Why don't you two investigate our new, er, new-ancient house while Mom and I get the furnace going?"

Jason and I began our tour outside, navigating around the house and gazing at it from every angle.

"It is truly gigantic, so that's got to be worth *something*," said Jason.

We ran to the backyard and contemplated the backside of the house. From the daylight basement to the dormer windows set against the sky, the house looked eerie.

Something caught my eye: a swirling movement in one of the upstairs windows.

"Did you see that?" I whispered.

"See what?"

"There," I said, pointing. "In that window."

"That's weird," he said. "It looks like someone is moving around up there. But...it must be Mom or Dad."

"No," I said, "*that* doesn't look like either of our parents. That person looks...transparent."

CHAPTER TWO

# Mabel

"You and your giant imagination!" scoffed Jason. "Come on, let's find out!"

We sprinted around to the front of the house. We found Mom and Dad sitting on the front porch having coffee.

"Were you upstairs just now?" I wheezed.

"Nope," said Mom. "We decided to

caffeinate before tackling the boxes."

Jason and I exchanged worried glances, but we didn't say anything.

"Why don't you two investigate your new rooms?" said Mom. "I think you'll be pleasantly surprised."

I was curious about my new room, but also weirdly nervous about what we might find. I couldn't get the thought of that transparent image out of my mind.

Jason and I climbed a wide wooden staircase up to the second floor. I

wondered how we'd know whose room was whose, but Mom had labeled each door with a name tag.

First, we passed a door with a label in Mom's handwriting: *Mom and Dad*. Next, we passed an unlabeled bathroom, a turquoise-blue room labeled *Anna*, and then a dark green room labeled *Jason*.

That left a single, lonely door at the far end of the hallway. I took a few steps closer and squinted at it. "I think

there's a label on that door," I said.

"Probably the bathroom," said Jason.

"Why would anyone label a bathroom? Plus, we already passed one."

I slowly walked toward the door at the end of the hallway. Jason followed close behind.

At first, I had a hard time deciphering the label. It was written in emerald green ink in an old-fashioned loopy cursive, and it read: *Mabel.*

It wasn't Mom's handwriting, and who on earth was Mabel?

"Doesn't Dad have a great-aunt Mabel?" asked Jason. "Maybe this is some sort of misguided Dad joke."

"Dad's jokes are usually just silly. This makes me feel creeped out, like someone else is in the house."

We cautiously backed away from the door and then turned on our heels, sprinted full-speed to the stairs, and ran out the front door.

Dad laughed at the panicked

expressions on our faces. "Looks like you two discovered an adventure—or maybe a misadventure found you."

"That was a mean trick," I huffed.

"What was?" asked Dad. He tilted his head sideways and scrunched up his face, like he was confused.

"We'll show you," I said. "Follow us."

We led Dad up the stairs and down the long hallway.

"It's gone!" I shouted. We searched the floor, but there was no sign of the *Mabel* label anywhere.

Dad walked away, muttering to himself. "I guess the joke's on me."

Jason and I stuck close to Mom and Dad for the rest of the morning. After lunch, we gathered our courage and went back upstairs to unpack boxes in our respective rooms.

I didn't want to be alone, so after a few minutes, I padded over to Jason's room.

"Can I help you unpack?" I asked.

"Sure," Jason agreed. After a minute, he said, "Let's play *try not to laugh*."

"Okay, but only if I get to go first."

I stood up and did my favorite silly dance—skipping with one step and then kicking a leg up and out to the side with the next step. "Welcome to the Land of Pigwingarovia, where pigs can fly!" I flapped my arms like wings.

"Are the pigs migrating?" asked Jason, and then we both doubled over with laughter.

# CHAPTER THREE

# Mystery Tea Party

After a few more rounds of the game, I begged Jason to help unpack in my room.

As we stepped through my doorway, a chilly blast of air hit me, as if a window had been left wide open. I opened my mouth to say "Brr," but before my breath could escape my lips, I saw it. All of my stuffed animals had been unpacked, dressed up, and arranged in a circle around my china tea set. It was a fluffy tea party!

"Wow," said Jason, "It looks like Mom went all out!"

But I knew Mom hadn't taken the time to unpack my china tea set or dress up my fluffies when there was so much to do.

This was weird! I shivered and backed out of the room.

I left Jason and sprinted down the hallway. Keeping one hand on the railing to keep from toppling, I barreled down the stairs, shrieking, "Mom!"

Mom hurried through the front door as I leapt down the final few steps. "What on earth is wrong, Anna?"

"Something strange is going on in my room! Come upstairs and see!"

Mom followed me up the stairs, muttering something about the "character and charm of an older home."

In my room, she saw the fluffy tea

party. "That is absolutely adorable," she said. "But Anna, I don't have time for jokes right now, and your china tea set might get broken."

"Mom, it wasn't me!" I said.

As she left my room, Mom said over her shoulder, "Enough joking around. You kids get your rooms unpacked."

I watched her walk away, wondering, *Now what*?

"Good one, Anna." Jason poked his head out from his bedroom doorway.

"I swear I didn't set up that tea party, and I don't think Mom…"

"No, not that," Jason said, "MY room! When did you have time to do it?"

*Huh?* I thought. *I didn't do anything to Jason's room.* I followed him into his room to see what he was talking about.

On the left side of the room, Jason's mattress leaned against one wall, surrounded by the disassembled pieces of his bed and a bunch of cardboard boxes. Two big suitcases stood next to the mattress. A third, smaller suitcase was on its side, unzipped.

"What?" I shrugged my shoulders at Jason. He nodded toward the other side of the room.

I followed his gaze to the window. It had a strange curtain. That surprised me because I didn't think Mom and Dad had unpacked the curtains yet. I took a step forward to get a closer look.

Wait!

Gross!

"Is that YOUR UNDERWEAR?" I couldn't get the question out without laughing.

Jason cracked up, too. "How'd you get them to stay up there?"

"It wasn't me. I've been with you all this time."

Suddenly, all of the underwear fell to the floor.

"MABEL?" we both yelled.

# CHAPTER FOUR

# Dancing Towels

Jason and I ran downstairs again. We stopped when we reached the sunny safety of the kitchen.

"We think Mabel is here, and she is not human," I announced to Jason. "This house is haunted!"

Jason searched through a box labeled *pantry* to find a snack to calm his nerves. He found a box of cheese crackers. "Let's just keep playing *try not to laugh* to take our minds off Mabel," he said.

Jason stood up and looked off into space while scratching the top of his head. I knew he was trying to think of something that would have me howling with laughter.

That's when a stack of dish towels rose a few inches into the air.

"Yikes!" Jason gasped.

I jumped and shrieked, "Did that just happen? Am I dreaming?" I pinched my arm and closed and opened my eyes.

The towels twisted around each other to form a little doll. The little towel arms and little towel legs started kicking and wind-milling. It was dancing.

"AAAH!" Jason and I screamed in unison.

We stared with wide-eyed wonder, until Jason said, "I think it's doing your

favorite silly dance…"

We looked at each other and began to laugh. This time, we didn't run out of the room.

Dad came in through the back door. The towels dropped before he entered the room. They fell into a perfectly folded pile.

"Aren't you two supposed to be unpacking?" asked Dad.

"You'd better not still be joking around," Mom said leaning in from the living room. "You can prank us *after* we finish unpacking."

"The ghost, Mabel, made these towels dance," I wheezed, pointing to the neat pile.

Mom and Dad exchanged a look that said, *Can you believe this?*

Jason chimed in, "I know it sounds like a joke, but I saw the towels dancing, too. It would've been hilarious if it weren't so freaky. Oh, and my underwear was hanging up in my room."

CHAPTER FIVE

# I Made You Laugh

Dad sighed dramatically and said, "Let's see this underwear art."

We walked in silence out of the kitchen and up the stairs. When we passed my bedroom door, I drew in a sharp breath.

"Wait, look!"

Theodora, my giant stuffed panda,

was now dressed up in Mom's clothes, and Felix, Jason's giant stuffed dog, was dressed up in Dad's clothes. All the details were so perfectly Mom-and-Dad-like that, in spite of my fear, the sight made me giggle.

"This is great!" Dad started laughing. He petted *Dog Dad* on the head. "You've never looked so good!"

Jason and I joined the laughter.

Dad noticed my cell phone sitting

on top of a box. "One quick pic, then you really need to get to work on these rooms." He took a selfie next to his dog self. "Make sure you put our clothes back."

As Dad walked downstairs, we could hear him still chuckling.

Just then, I got a text:

> Jason and Anna
> I made you laugh!
> Now, it's your turn to make me laugh.
> —Mabel

"She just wants to play with us!" I shouted. "But how will we know if we make her laugh?"

"Whoo hoo, hahaha," she cackled from a distance. It sounded like the wind, but I knew it was Mabel.

Who knew a ghost could have such a fantastic sense of humor?

# About Us

## The Author

Gabrielle Snyder writes for both children and adults. She loves reading all kinds of stories, especially ghost stories. When she's not reading or writing, she loves taking nature walks, visiting Little Free Libraries, and baking sweet treats with her kids. She lives in Oregon with her family, including one dog and one dog-like cat.

## The Illustrator

James Rey Sanchez's love of art came from countless hours of reading comics, playing video games, and watching Saturday morning cartoons. He looks forward to showing the world what he can do with a fluid and unique style, expressive characters, and beautiful colors.